The Giant Apple

The Giant Apple

by Ursel Scheffler

illustrations by Silke Brix-Henker

Carolrhoda Books, Inc./Minneapolis

Translated from the German by Amy Gelman.

Library of Congress Cataloging-in-Publication Data

Scheffler, Ursel.
[Riesenapfel. English]
The giant apple / by Ursel Scheffler :
illustrations by Silke Brix-Henker :
[translated from the German by Amy Gelman].
p.   cm.
Translation of : Der Riesenapfel.
Summary: In their quest to win a prize at the harvest festival, the residents of Appleville neglect
their crops in order to grow a giant apple and
discover during the winter that fame and honor do
not fill empty stomachs.

ISBN 0-87614-413-X (lib. bdg.)
[1. Apple—Fiction. 2. Contests—Fiction. 3.
Farm life—Fiction.] I. Brix-Henker, Silke, ill.
II. Title.
PZ7.S3425Gi   1990   89-23888
[E]—dc20   CIP
                                                 AC

Manufactured in the United States of America

1 2 3 4 5 6 7 8 9 10 99 98 97 96 95 94 93 92 91 90

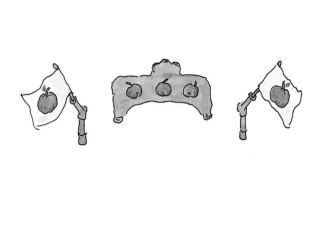

High in the sunny mountains sits a little town called Appleville. Further down the mountain, on the other side of the stream, is a town called Beet Valley.

Every year, without fail, the farmers of both villages would bring their finest vegetables to the Harvest Festival. And every year, without fail, the farmers of Beet Valley would win the grand prize for the best and biggest vegetables.

This year was no different — the potatoes from Beet Valley were enormous, and they won the contest easily. While the farmers from Beet Valley danced a happy jig, the farmers of Appleville were stomping mad.

"Something must be done!" declared Appleville's mayor.

The Appleville farmers met
to discuss the matter.

"It makes my blood boil," said
one farmer, "but I don't see how
we can beat them. The rich soil in their
valley will always grow better vegetables than
our rocky soil ever will."

"Well, that's true," said the mayor. "But, then again,
the sun shines on our hills long after the valley is
in shadow. And that's good for growing apples."

"Our apples *are* delicious," said another farmer, "but
they're not spectacular like the Beet Valley potatoes."

"They could be if we took extra-special care of them," said the mayor thoughtfully. He was very young and had just returned from farming school. He was also very clever, which is why he was elected mayor.

The mayor called a meeting in the town hall and proposed a plan. Appleville would do everything possible to grow the biggest apple ever seen. It would be so big, so rosy, so *splendid*, it would make the Beet Valley farmers turn green with envy.

The people of Appleville thought
that was a great idea. Soon they
talked of nothing else. They forgot
about their other crops and tried
to remember everything they could
about growing apples. Every day
they met in the orchard to discuss
their plan. First they cut down all
the apple trees except one. That
way, the chosen tree would get every
bit of sunlight in the sky, and its
roots would get every bit of water
in the ground. Then they fertilized
the tree with a secret formula that
the mayor had concocted.

In the spring, the tree burst into bloom. The townspeople brought hundreds of bees to the orchard to fertilize the blossoms. When the first little knots of fruit appeared on the branches, the town's brass band played a concert to welcome them.

Then they picked all the apples except one, so that the chosen apple would get every drop of sap from the tree.

Soon the apple was huge! Some of the tree's branches had to be cut out of the way, and others had to be propped up so the tree wouldn't collapse.

The townspeople talked endlessly about the miraculous fruit and the glory it would bring to Appleville. They posted a guard at the orchard gate so outsiders wouldn't discover their secret. The mayor even moved his bed into the orchard so he could keep the night watch himself.

As the apple's cheeks turned a rosy red, it began to smell wonderfully sweet. The women of Appleville sewed their bridal veils together end-to-end to protect the apple from the insects that hovered around it.

By September, the apple was a giant red-and-green jewel.

At last Harvest Day arrived. At the crack of dawn, the townspeople assembled in the orchard. They sawed off the stem and slid the apple gently onto an ox cart. When they realized it was too big to fit through the orchard gate, they tore the gate down. Then they carefully polished the apple until it shone.

Everyone quickly changed into their finest clothes and gathered for their parade. The people of Appleville were a sight to behold as they marched down the road to Beet Valley.

Along the way, they announced their approach with a blast of trumpets.

All the festival judges agreed that the giant apple was the most magnificent fruit they'd ever seen and awarded it the gold medal. The newspaper took a picture of the mayor, and word of the giant apple spread throughout the countryside. The people of Appleville returned to their village in triumph and celebrated for three days straight.

When the excitement had died down, they wondered what they should do with the giant apple. The mayor suggested building a museum to display the apple. The villagers imagined people from all over the world traveling to see their apple and got right to work on the new building.

Appleville
Apple Museum

By the time the frost came, however, brown spots appeared on the giant apple, and it began to rot. The mayor suggested making dried fruit of it, but the people wondered who would come to see an old, dried-up slice of fruit. They stopped working on the museum and wondered what to do next.

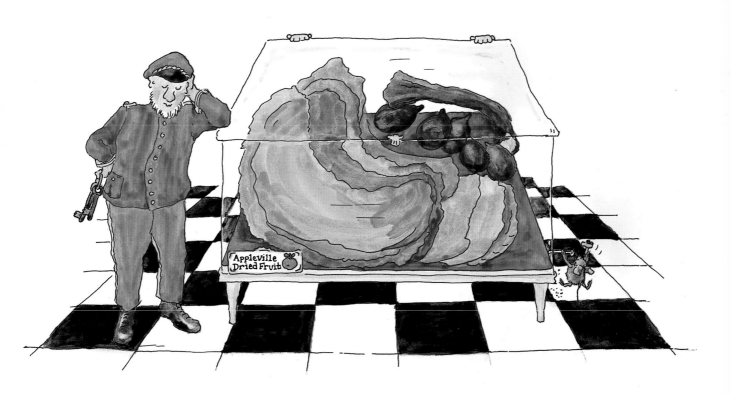

"Well," said the mayor, "I guess there's just one thing left to do—we'll have to eat it."

So the townspeople made 285 jars of applesauce and 32 barrels of apple juice. The
children ate so many apple pies, apple donuts,
and apple fritters that they ran and hid if they
even so much as smelled an apple.

As the weather grew colder, the villagers realized they had forgotten to store any vegetables for the winter. Their cellars were bare, and they were very tired of applesauce.

They needed to have vegetables for the long winter—and everyone knew who grew the best vegetables in the mountains.

The farmers of Appleville scraped together all their savings to buy vegetables from the farmers of Beet Valley.

Trudging down the road to Beet Valley, the villagers thought about the giant apple and what it had meant to them. It had brought them glory, that's for certain. But they had also learned that the winter would be mighty long living on glory and applesauce alone.